James & The smiling planet

Marilena Pappa

ISBN: 9798703117323

JAMES & THE SMILING PLANET
MARILENA PAPPA

1ST ENGLISH EDITION: FEBRUARY 2021

TITLE: JAMES & THE SMILING PLANET

AUTHOR: MARILENA PAPPA

COVER/ ILLUSTRATION: MARILENA PAPPA

SPECIAL THANKS TO

KONSTANTINA STAMOULI & LINA LABRIANAKI

CONTENTS

Chapter 1
God Varvas' mess

James: I hate that snotty Mandy! What is it that she wants and she's after me all day long?

James' mom: What are you talking about, my son? Mandy considers you as her best friend! She cares about you!

Mandy: James, where are you?

That's how our heroes' life went by until one icy spring morning arrived and God Varvas (enormous as a five-storey apartment building and black as the midnight sky) wanted to play a little bit with the threads that define people's lives. Every thread represented a human life. You can only imagine how the universe was full of threads!

Huge and colorful, spanning to the infinity. Countless strings in which God Varvas rested his fingers and played the melodies of the air, the rustling of the leaves, the wave on the shores.

He was playing and was creating the most beautiful songs in the world. He was feeling happy that we could create the most unique sounds. He was playing until he accidentally cut one without wanting to. He then tried to re-stick it with some saliva and pink gum, but his effort was in vain. The thread had already been cut and the piece that connected the two cut ends had evaporated somewhere on Earth. In a place where the creatures of the universe are not allowed to enter, so that people do not realize their existence.

So, God Varvas leaned on Earth to see all the sorrow and pain he had caused. He fell upon the sky and darkened it with his black tears painting every white cloud black. Exactly how little James' soul went dark.

Ever since that day James doesn't talk to anyone, he doesn't laugh, he doesn't play basketball – the game he loved so much. He only remembers his dad's red thread and cries.

James' mom stands strong, but she is crying at nights and blames the unfair fate that stole away her husband.

Mandy stays home sad. She's only thinking of her friend. James doesn't talk to anyone since the day of his big basketball game. She recalls that day and smiles. It was the most beautiful day of her life.

She was sitting in the gray stands of her school, wearing her favorite orange dress, waiting for the big game to start.

It was the first time that James was playing a key role in the school basketball team. She wore the best dress she had and

prayed that her beloved friend would do well and succeed many baskets in order to give a good lesson to Tasos, the leader of the team who was making fun of him.

As a matter of fact, once, Mandy, was so irritated that Tasos and the rest of the boys had scattered James' books in the schoolyard, had thrown a whole handful of itchy dust into their bags. The whole school then laughed at them.

Finally, James appeared. He was wearing the gray-yellow school uniform and looked like a prince in her eyes. Mandy started shouting at him to wish him good luck, but he continued to move towards the coach's bench, ignoring her.

After forty minutes of hard game, Tasos passes the ball to James three seconds before the end of the half time and while his team was one point behind the opponent. Without thinking, James shoots and becomes the hero of the game.

While God Varvas, was holding the blue thread of James and the red of his dad, accidentally pulls the second a little more than he should and breaks it.

Chapter 2
Varvas & Coumara

That night little James could not sleep. Strong wind hit the windows and turned back into the dark sky. In the distant universe, in the unknown, God Varvas was sitting on the top of the moon, painting the stars and sighing heavily. He was blowing in and blowing out and was wondering what to do. After his last blunder, witch Coumara said to Sun, God Varvas father:

- I have to rule people's lives now. Don't you see the mess that stupid Varvas has caused? He should not stay in this position any longer.

But Sun, wise enough to know that witch Coumara had evil plans for the fortunes of mortals, gave God Varvas a year to redress and prove to Galaxy that he did not hold this position just because he was his son. Otherwise Sun couldn't do anything else but hand over the position to the insidious Coumara. The majority of Planets and Asteroids of the Universe had already begun to whisper and talk about Varvas' inadequacy.

This is what the son of Sun was thinking when he saw witch Coumara with her filthy broomstick braided by filthy, stale coumarins arriving from planet Kazan.

- What are you doing here, witch Coumara? You belong to Kazan, the Land of the Damned. The land where no juicy and red coumarins grow, only dirty and disgusting like those in your broomstick. Where the residents are rotten human beings who live only to serve you.

- My place, you idiot, is here. You are just a useless person who rules the world thanks to your father. In a year from now when I will become the ascendant of the Earth, everything will change. I will destroy this stupid planet, and, in its place, I will create planet Hazair. A new planet full coumarins to feed myself. To stay young and fresh forever. And I will turn these stupid human beings who inhabit the Earth into Khazars. In the place of their minds I will place tiny kernels and I´ll use them as my slaves. They will pick up the coumarin harvest and hand it over to me.

- You are making a terrible mistake Coumara. I will not let any of this happen. I will find the solution and then I will kick you out of this Galaxy. You will be forever exiled in the ninth dimension.

- We will see this you fool. Oh, and don´t bother to paint stars. In a year from now everything will be dark. Earth will be a cold planet with greenhouses only for coumarins. You and your dad will go where you came from. I ´ve had enough of you for so many years.

Ha, ha, ha… and her evil laughter echoed throughout the vastness of space as she walked away. And God Varvas was left alone to look at the stars he painted and to regret his recklessness. Alone at the top of the Moon

Chapter 3

One blunder after another

Today the stars worked overtime because God Varvas fell asleep at the top of the Moon and forgot to extinguish them, he forgot to paint the day and Sun alone could not illuminate the Earth.

So, when little James got up to get ready for school, he got confused since it was still night. Just like all the other inhabitants of the Earth, were confused.

The celestial bodies of the Universe, pretty upset, convened an emergency council to deal with the crisis.

Sun sat first at the table. With his head down, he heard planet Brasuvius talking about his son's inability to carry out his duties as Earth's Ruler. God Varvas tried to interrupt twice but his dad's rays burned him to stop. He knew he was wrong. Comet Lampson proposed that someone had to supervise God Varvas until the one-year suspension expires.

At the end of the huge black round table that hovered in the infinity, witch Coumara was smiling wickedly. She knew that she would be the one to supervise God Varvas and therefore she would make his life as miserable as possible. And so, it happened. All the celestial bodies voted for the abominable witch for the position of supervisor and Sun, despite its opposition, could not react.

When the council ended and Sun was left alone with his son, God Varvas enraged by the council's decision, began to accuse the celestial bodies of ignorance for what he had offered for so long as Earth's Ruler.

Sun was listening at him accusing anyone else but himself and remained silent. Only when he was over, he told him:

- Child, do not accuse others of ignorance when you, by yourself with your current actions have underestimated your work so far. You have disappointed us all, but most of all you have disappointed your best self. You are to lose your position and leave the planet at the mercy of ruthless Coumara. Do not forget that the mistakes of your predecessors cost your mother's life. So much pain, so much sorrow could have been avoided if the previous Earth's Ruler was less irresponsible.

These were the last words of Sun and he got up from his imposing red throne and with a heavy flight returned to the sky. Today Sun would not shine. You thought a cloud had covered his bright eyes and flooded them with tears.

God Varvas, after extinguishing the huge round table and the innumerable red chairs with his intergalactic eraser, headed to the depths of the sky immersed in his thoughts.

When he reached the most recondite part of the vast blue planet and his green eyes could see nothing but the vast, blue dimension he painted with his hands massive white clouds and hid behind them so that no one could see his tears flow in his black body. It felt like then. When his mother, Goddess Salva, disappeared.

Chapter 4
Inside Varvas' mind

God Varvas must have been thirteen centuries old (very small considering that the average life span is a hundred centuries) when the name of the gloomy witch Araba was first heard. Witch Arab who travelled from distant galaxies wanted to bring innovations and of course to become the ruler of the Earth. The green planet as the aliens called it or the planet that smiles. Its value competed even to that of the ancient planet Pintura, the colorful planet that no longer exists.

On planet Pintura, inhabited by creatures with special spiritual sharpness, Sun found refuge at a time when a huge galactic rain was threatening to extinguish his rays and destroy him forever. This is also the place where he met Goddess Salva, he fell in love with her and married her. At the time when Goddess Salva gave birth to God Varvas, the three Fates were on vacation in the solar galaxy. When they learned that Sun had a successor, they went to give their blessings to the young God.

Fate Arianna went to the crib and looked at the little black God. She smiled at him and then said to Goddess Salva: your son will become famous all over Galaxy but remember... Parents must be sacrificed for their children. Never forget it.

Then, she made a turn and her majestic purple cape covered her and the other Fates and made them disappear.

However, no one commented on Arianna's words, although she had predicted the upcoming end. So, when little Varvas turned thirteen centuries old and witch Araba was intriguing for a place in the dominion of the Earth, the Earth's Ruler Kokoronos decided to take a trip to planet Pintura. Witch Araba, knowing that Goddess Salva would be there, pretended she was in love with the naive Kokoronos in order to take her with him. The innocent planet, madly in love with her, not only decided to take her to planet Pintura, but also to marry her.

Outrageous, the universe decided to strike in order to calm the mindless Earth's Ruler. No means of transportation would work for a week. And so, Sun covered his rays with a huge dark cape lent to him by the Night because everything worked with solar energy. And darkness fell on the Earth. Something that of course did not deter Kokoronos who, enchanted by the spells of witch Araba, was persuaded to camouflage himself and travel with the broomstick of his insidious husband.

During this time panic has spread on Earth due to the total solar eclipse as some scientists called it and all people terrified thought that this would be the end of the world. Meanwhile all planets of the universe were looking for the newlywed couple across the galaxy. But they were so well camouflaged that when planet Pintura searched inside him did not find anything suspicious. Yet Kokoronos and Araba had already arrived.

They remained hidden for thirteen days under the ground of planet Pintura, during which witch Araba became pregnant.

On the fifteenth day, the witch craved for coumarins, so the baby's parents decided that when it was born, they would baptize it Coumaro or Coumara. After a month, it was time for witch Araba to give birth. She took the baby out of her mouth (this is how all witches usually give birth) and saw an all-yellow creature just like her, with two black eyeballs and pink hair. She hugged her and said:

- My love, together we will destroy the Earth. Baby Coumara instead of crying like all the other babies, started laughing with an eerie, whispery, almost scary laugh.

Three days later, while Goddess Salva was putting little Varvas to bed with colorful brushes flying above him and creating beautiful visions, witch Araba invaded the all-white tower where the family stayed. She kidnapped both, trapping them in a magic circle. She then transferred them to the depths of planet Pintura.

Then she went to Sun and said to him:

-If you want to see this filthy Goddess Salva and your little spoiled child again, you have to divorce her and marry me. Then you will exile them to the ninth dimension. This is the only way they will stay alive. And of course, I will become the leader of the Earth.

Sun was so furious that he hit her with his rays and burnt her hair.

You're not going to get away with it easily, said Araba angrily as she picked up her glowing pink tufts floating in space. She later reached the depths of planet Pintura and ordered Kokoronos to stop giving food to their prisoners. He could not refuse since witch Araba had given him the most valuable gift, their daughter, witch Coumara.

Fourteen whole days passed by. Fourteen days during which the entire universe searched for the missing ones. Fourteen days where Kokoronos threatened his friends and family not to reveal to Sun where his family is. Fourteen days during which little Varvas and his mom starved.

On the fifteenth day Goddess Salva could no longer bear to see her child slowly dying. She took off the gold ornament with which she had gathered her silky black long hair and made the first gash in her white glass skin. She was in unbearable pain, but she stifled her pain so as not to frighten her baby. From the initial incision he made the milk rolled, since all gods instead of blood in their veins have white fragrant milk.

He made little Varvas drink till he was full. Then Goddess Salva fell asleep exhausted and her soul left her body and found herself in the universe. She went to planet Pintura and told him:

- Save my son. I must go now.

Then she climbed the highest stair of the universe, and before she leaped into the white orb of Souls, looked down searching for her husband, and cried with all the strength she had left: my Sun, my love, farewell forever.

Sun, who was on the Comet Lampson and was exploring it, heard his wife's voice and ran to catch her. But she was already lost. He couldn't believe he let his wife die. All he could think now was that he should save his son. And he flew up to planet Pintura to ask if he had seen Salva, and if she had told him anything about little Varvas.

But planet Pintura who had not heard the last words of the goddess but only saw her soul disappear, began to languish and weep because Goddess Salva was the pride of the universe. She was one of the best creatures ever existed. Everything that was colorful in him turned into dark, everything that was alive and happy died forever. Just before Sun could reach him, planet Pintura petrified the vegetation inside him, and with a mighty clench it broke and became millions of colorless pieces. Its inhabitants scattered over the universe and died.

Sun seeing this chaotic situation began to search among the debris for survivors and also for the core of the planet to bring him back to life. He searched for days with the rest of the planets, until a small reddish light began to shine through the rubble. He ran to catch it and digging deeper caught sight of his son cuddling with little Coumara. They had both eaten the core of the planet to survive, and all that was left was this little red piece.

Sun was so moved to have found his son again, he began to cry, as a result of which one of his hundred huge golden-yellow rays was extinguished. Since then Sun illuminates the earth with ninety-nine rays, so in some places it is day and in others Night.

He caught God Varvas and squeezed him so hard that his longing almost choked him, and he said to him:

- My Son, now we'll be together forever. I will never leave you alone again. Never, never. They remained hugged together for hours, weeping and bidding farewell to Goddess Salva.

But no one commented on the fact that the two children had eaten the core of planet Pintura.

In the following days a council was convened to decide the fate of little Coumara after her parents were also killed in the Great Disaster. It was decided to send her to her mother's homeland where she would be taken over by her infernal cousin, witch Ploumada. As for the core of planet Pintura, it was a common secret that it would give special color abilities to both children. They would only have to learn to use them properly.

That is why Sun devoted his life to teaching his son that the gift given to him did not give him the right to interfere in the lives of others except for good. So, the Little God learned very early that he could paint and color the whole universe but only to bring joy to the inhabitants of the Galaxy.

On the contrary, witch Ploumada often used the abilities of witch Coumara for self-interest, regardless of whether this harmed the lives of others around her. Thus, witch Coumara learned to paint to destroy, while God Varvas only to create a world more beautiful.

Sun was always so proud of God Varvas. Every night he was looking above at the orb of Souls and was whispering:

- Don't worry, my love. Be proud of our son. He went to sleep alone, but always having with him the thought of Goddess Salva.

Chapter 5

Back to the reality

This is what God Varvas was thinking about, and his tears flooded the clouds which he drew to hid behind them. They got so bloated that they started crying too.

On Earth a terrible storm broke out. It lasted two days during which God Varvas stayed hidden behind the washed-out clouds, while witch Coumara took over the duties of Earth's Ruler after Varvas was missing.

Little James down on Earth, watched the rain lashing furiously the trees and he cried too. When Mandy went to visit him, he said to her:

-Go away, you´re not my friend. I´m all alone.

Mandy ran away and fell into a puddle of mud and tore her favorite orange dress.

After two weeks and while God Varvas remained hidden, the situation on Earth got worse and worse because witch Coumara was painting every day a new disaster. Earthquakes, volcanoes and huge waves were hitting every corner of the globe, almost every day. And from afar Sun looked down upon the Earth with melancholy, as the planet was weeping, and its ever-present smile had been extinguished. He shouted to his son to come back if he could hear him. The voice of Sun reached to the ends of the Galaxy, but God Varvas closed his ears not to hear a thing.

Three days later God Varvas had his body so soaked in tears that his black color began to fade away. He grew dull. He was so tired that in a minute he fell asleep.

There, in the land of the dreams he walked miles. He crossed snow-capped mountains, tropical forests, plunged into lakes and rivers, until he reached the dividing line with the orb of Souls. In the blurred window that stood in front and distinguished the false from the spiritual he discerned a familiar figure. He stuck his head against the wet glass and stared at Goddess Salva staring at him and crying.

They stayed like that for hours. Then Goddess Salva began to write with her finger on the blurred glass:

-To survive you must sacrifice many things. Take care, my son.

And just like that Goddess Salva disappeared. The same moment God Varvas opened his green eyes and looked around him. He had made up his mind. He had thought this through on his long dream-journey.

Meanwhile, witch Coumara continued undaunted painting catastrophic events. In the last few days, she discovered a new trick to spread evil on Earth. she painted the iniquity. She dipped her huge transparent brush into the palette of colors of envy, malice and rage and in due proportion created as much of it as she wanted. Then she shook the brush over the Earth, and from afar dripped the color of iniquity where it pleased her. So, people without knowing why felt an overpowering desire to destroy and kill, and that's what they did.

Within a week Coumara had turned everybody against each other. Shops and houses were destroyed while fear spread everywhere. People watched the events unfazed and wondered about the sequel. The witch from above was smiling because she knew that in a little while everyone carried away by fear would rely on the first person who would present himself as a savior. And then she would choose an earthly creature, make them her slave, and set them to rule the world. Her dream of destroying the planet and turning it into a vast expanse of coumarins would take shape. Everyone would live under the regime of terror, killing Democracy, while she will obtain full power.

At the end of the nightmarish week for Earth, Democracy, knowing that Coumara desired her complete annihilation, rose from her majestic white throne and walked to Sun to ask him for help. When she reached him, she saw a Sun dark and feeble. He had stopped eating for days. He felt responsible for the downfall of the Earth.

Sun, who was surprised by her presence, began to shine strangely. He made room for her on the long glass bench for her to sit and asked her what she wanted.

- Sun, people have forgot about me and want to kick me out of the Universe. They have forgot the importance of my existence and how much they can accomplish through me. Over the past few years, they have neglected me. This is why Coumara found fertile ground to sow hatred and discord among people. Sun, you have to help me.

Sun, who knew that everything Democracy said was true, with his rays bowed told her:

- I'm afraid there's nothing I can do. All the celestial bodies have voted for Coumara. Only one could help but it seems he is unable to bear the burden of his responsibilities and he is hiding. Return to your throne and await the end. That's what I'll do. In the future, you and I will be nothing more than a memory.

So, Democracy turned back to her throne in despair of the unjust end that awaited her.

Chapter 6
The great decision

The next morning God Varvas got up before Sun had set. He didn't want anyone to notice him. Everything had to be done in absolute secrecy. Because if his dad knew what he was about to do, he wouldn't have allowed it.

So, he rose from his clouds and walked the path that the stars formed to the Earth. He made sure to step on tiptoe, so he wouldn't wake any of them. No one was to be seen. But little Asterius, who wasn't a great sleeper when he lighted the Earth, was awakened by a step of God Varvas. So, she followed him to see where he was going. They both went to Earth together, to the part of the Atlantic Ocean where witch Coumara had fallen asleep. In order not to wake her up, God Varvas went the other way. Asterius watched the God being very nervous, taking deep breaths and wondering what he was about to do. Meanwhile he had extinguished his light and had become one with the night so that God wouldn't understand that he was watching him.

Everything during this moment were creating a composition of a dreamy landscape. Complete silence had spread everywhere, with the exception of course of the heavy snoring of the witch. It looked like as if a secret symphony of the universe was playing harmoniously the sound of the silence, while the whole galaxy had slept first. The stars looked like spilt magic dust that a divine hand had cast to soothe pain by magic. The great moment had arrived, anyone could feel that.

God Varvas was so anxious, he was shaking. Nevertheless, he took off his huge invisible bag a long telescope. With this he could see what was going on Earth. As he was looking to spot James' house, he heard a whisper behind him. He turned and saw a brown mass rising before him. It was the Fear that told him to leave. He was telling him that it was not worth sacrificing himself for the salvation of the planet, that he was no longer responsible since the bodies of the Galaxy preferred the witch. He told him more than that, and for a moment God Varvas put his telescope down and thought of leaving, of giving up. But a voice within hollered, " No, you will stay and finish what you began. You're not a coward."

This is what he did, and the Fear vanished. After an hour God Varvas finally spotted James. He was in his bed and sleeping heavily. He took his magic green marker and painted on this spot of the Earth a green dot. Then he packed up his things, tied them up and ate them. Together he swallowed the note with James' mission, so as the kid would understand what he had to do. Now it was time for the hardest part of all.

He placed his hands between his belly and began to pull it hard until it opened. When he finally made it, a red light flooded the universe. It was the core of planet Pintura glowing inside his stomach. Then he pulled it out of him and threw it with all the force he had left on the green dot. Exhausted and without the core of planet Pintura, without his tools and with a big hole on his belly that was constantly pouring milk, he turned to the clouds that he had painted before so that he could hide without anyone being able to perceive him. He was bound to die.

Asterius, shocked by what took place before his eyes, followed God Varvas to the ends of the sky and saw him lying in the white layers of the planet. He could not leave him like this.

He went above God's face and inhaled the aura of death that surrounded him. So, he gave him some time to live, during which Varvas would be in a coma. He had completely lost consciousness.

Meanwhile back to Earth, the stomach, with the tremendous force it hurled out, entered the room and then James´ body. James awoke instantly. He wasn't the same person anymore or at least he wasn't just the little James. He knew that now he had a purpose, a mission. He knew that he had to leave his home and go far, far to the ends of the world, to make him as it was before.

His mind automatically began to process the information he had received from God Varvas' letter, while his belly was literary boiling.

Suddenly James' hands were filled with colors, and the whole room was glowing bizarrely. The light coming from the window of the room pierced through the glass and reached the window of Mandy's room. In her sleep, and without understanding what she was doing, she rose and followed the light until she reached its source. The magic was so tremendous that it formed a passage through the glass, and Mandy stepped to the light and entered her friend's room. The room was flooded with colors since little James, infatuated by this new ability, could not stop painting for a moment. Mandy, who couldn't understand what she was doing, slipped on a thick layer of pink and did a reverse somersault before landing forcefully on the floor. From the shock she awoke and wondered what had happened.

James was so engrossed with the power he had acquired that he did not notice the presence of the little one there.

When he turned his face and saw her, he said:

- What are you doing here? When did you get in? How?

- Well, I don't know what happened. One minute I was asleep in my bed and the next I woke up here. What is that light coming out of your eyes? And why is the whole room filled with colors? James, what's going on?

- Let me tell you something, snot, I don't have time to explain. You can't tell anyone what you saw today, or Earth will be in danger because of you. I can't stay here any longer, I have a mission to accomplish, he said, and jumped out of the window.

- Wait, Where Are you going? I'm not leaving you alone.

- Forget about it.

- Well, then I'll tell everyone what I saw!

- You're such a nightmare! Ok, you can come. I'll take you with me, but you aren't allowed to talk whatsoever. Do you agree?

Mandy's excitement was so big that she ran to embrace James so fast, that they both fell down and smudged with paint.

- You started being stupid and we haven't even begun yet? James told her while he was throwing a layer of blue over him. Don't you have any brains to think?

This is how James and Mandy begun their journey, without knowing what was next...

Chapter 7

In a new world

A t dawn the children had already left the city and

reached the Green Valley of Kantiliri, following the instructions of God Varvas. When they got there James took a small dose of blue from his thumb and yellow from his forefinger. At first, he threw the blue color into the green trees across the valley, forming a blue bridge, and then over it the yellow one. In combination the two colors looked like green, so that no one could distinguish the magic bridge among the world of trees.

Mandy looked bewildered at her friend and wondered what was going on. How did James get so many colors? She looked at him again and again, yet she did not ask him anything as she didn´t want them to fight any more. So, she followed him as on the bridge without saying a word. It was not until they had entered the vastness of tree branches that she said to him:

- James, can I hold your hand? I'm scared.

- Oh, you girls! Anyway, ok, hold my hand. But be careful not to throw me down again, he said, and caught her by the arm.

As they went deeper and deeper, they could discern flashes among the leaves, and hear a whisper growing louder. When they arrived, the eyes of the two children were flooded by the images of a huge fair with thousands of toys, colorful wheels that could take you to the sky, carts that collided, trains that flew to the clouds. The atmosphere smelled like sugar and caramelized peanuts. On the toys, little elves threw magic moon dust to work, while almost most of them were dwarfs.

The children marched along the fair enchanted by the festive atmosphere. On their right they discerned a little corridor leading to the queerest circus they had ever seen.

Elephants as small as mice flew to the highest point of the circus, while giant butterflies swung before the astonished eyes of the spectators. Fires, applause and laughter.

Everything was strange in this mysterious city. Even time flowed differently. Mandy noticed that from one side of the sky the color had already begun to get dark and the time was only eight o'clock in the morning! By the time she turned her eyes to the other side the sky had become black. And darkness spread everywhere. Everything was suddenly illuminated by a huge pointed clock that lit automatically. Within two minutes it was midnight, and the clock began to tick furiously.

At the sound of it the spectators stood up dumbfounded, and so did the merchants. Panic was spread as everyone was running like a maniac. In the midst of this tumult the two surprised children headed for an unknown gate. They ran for miles through the darkness and finally reached an embalmed forest.

The birds, the trees, the inhabitants, all were motionless. Across the forest stood a large wooden sign entitled: "The backstage". Only at the other edge of the forest a light flickered in a purple hut. Without having any other choice, James and Mandy moved on. Their feet were filled with blue and gold gleaming dust, since instead of soil the ground was braided with thick layers of magic sand.

Outside the hut Mandy's heart was beating loudly from anguish. She was almost hung on her little friend who seemed more composed than she did. Although James was feeling as unprotected as Mandy, nevertheless he did not hesitate to push the door with one move and enter.

The first thing he saw was a strange woman. Her hair was white, and her skin formed small rotating golden circles. Her age was undetermined. Not young, not old. The same could be said of her beauty. She looked like the most beautiful creature ever, and as soon as you looked at her again her countenance grew ugly and dull. She seemed as she was taken out of a fairy tale. So did her house, which inwardly extended to infinity and was painted all black, making a contrast with all the objects that were all white. When her eyes met that of the children, she said to them:

- What are you doing here? You've lost your way, haven't you?

The children, transfixed by the erratic image, just nodded to affirm.

- Sit down, she told them. You will certainly be hungry. With a curious snap of her fingers the white table in the hall was filled with beautiful, strange colored sweets. The two children began to taste all the dishes, filling their mouths with exquisite flavors.

Then the strange woman asked:

- Has God Varvas sent you? Without his approval the access of mortals here is forbidden.

Mandy who was almost feeling the questions pouring out of her mouth, couldn't restrain herself no longer and said:

- Where are we? Why does this forest seem to me so different from all the others?

- Oh, Mandy, you don't know anything, do you? You are on the other side of the planet. You're at the Earth's backstage. This is the place where they bring all the defective creatures. Especially those that do not obey the tick of the Great Clock. They are petrified and transported here until they come to their senses. This used to be the case with humans, but then witch Araba invented the prisons.

They are the backstage of Life. Here it grows the magic dust that sets all the mechanisms of the planet in motion. If you stay till the morning you will see the dwarfs gather it up in large glass jars. Then they share part of it with each other and send the rest to the human side of the Earth so that people can start their cars, cook and generally make any machine work. Something, of course, that you call electricity, because that is the form it takes when it enters your side.

- Why aren't you stoned like everyone else here?

- I, my little girl, I am Life. Everything around you, even you yourself, is a part of me. I supervise and regulate everything. As for God Varvas, James will explain better to you. He knows him better than anyone. And she looked at James with a smile.

Mandy, even more confused, she looked at her friend's eyes and then Life and finally responded:

- Where should we go now? What should we do?

- Your friend already knows that. He will guide you now. But as far as I can tell, your next stop will be the city of tears. Be careful, and take these, too, otherwise you will freeze, she said, and gave them two woolen coats.

- Good luck, and James don't be afraid to go to the end. God Varvas lives inside you and helps you.

James, who had been watching for so long without speaking, took from his hands some gold dust which he had gathered in the street, and with a delicate move he created a small beautiful rose.

Then he said to Life:

- As the rose grows and blooms you will know that we are well. If it withers, it means that something bad has happened to us and we need your help urgently.

Then James grabbed Mandy by the arm and pulled her out.

- Let's go. we have a long way to go.

The two children began to walk again. After half an hour Mandy couldn't stand it no longer and said:

- If you don't tell me now who God Varvas is, where we're going and why you're taking colors off your hands, I'm not going anywhere.

And she sat down on the silver grass waiting for an answer.

James, furious for the delay, told her:

- I don't have time for this. You're the one that followed me, and I'm dragging you with me. Stay here if you want. I'm leaving. I can't deal with your immaturity. And he just disappeared behind the trees.

Mandy, sitting in the dark, alone and frightened like never before in an unknown world, blamed herself. At daybreak Sun found her weeping. Until…

- You're still here?

Mandy turned to see if it was who she thought it was. James had returned to take her with him.

- Come on. What are you doing? he asked her, and with a gesture wiped the tears from her cheeks.

- Let's go and I'll explain everything to you on the way, he said, and blew her a kiss on the cheek. At the same moment the rose in Life's house lost something of its glow.

Meanwhile in another part of the forest the real James was walking nervous and confused. All he could think of was little Mandy. How was it possible, now that he had got rid of her, to think only of her?

Choked by his thoughts and guilt, he turned back to find her. But when he arrived, it was too late. Mandy had disappeared. He had left with the" new " James.

Our little hero searched all around, but Mandy was nowhere to be found. He went back to Life's house in case he had seen her. But Life was gone, and the house was empty. Not knowing what else he to do, he started walking again towards the city of tears. Perhaps on the way he would meet his little friend.

At the other side of the forest, Mandy was walking carelessly without being able to explain her friend's sudden change. They were heading to the city of tears, too. From a different gate than the one of James.

After an hour's walk our little hero arrived outside the bronze door leading to the city sanctuaries. Having in his mind all the time Mandy, he entered the city. At the same time, from a different entrance, Mandy with the "new" James, were opening the gate for the world of tears.

Chapter 8
The city of tears

Mandy's eyes blinked curiously when he saw the city. It was a city made of tears. The tears of the people waiting to be shed. A city transparent and frozen. Because of the freeze the tears had solidified and formed houses, cars, and in the center of the city an unbelievable towering sacred building with pointed ledges. Every corner of it was carved with strange melancholy designs and extended as far as the sky. Even the ground was made of tears. One could distinguish the fishes swimming. A melancholy roar was diffusing throughout the city. It was like voices wailing.

As they continued their tour, a tree collapsed in front of the children's eyes after tears broke and all became water spilled on the ground. Mandy asked her friend what all this meant, and "James" replied that a man had just cried somewhere on Earth. Every minute something was crumbling in this city, and something new was being made of new tears that were waiting to be shed.

Only the sacred building remained unscathed. It was laid for many centuries and grew day by day. In particular lately its extent had greatly increased. Even more, from the day that witch Coumara became Earth's Ruler, every second new peaks of tears were added. In a few teardrops you could discern strange creatures moving or sitting and gazing in vain, with empty eyes, at absolute nothingness.

As they continued walking, Mandy looked up between the tears of the sacred building, and all she could see was her and James embraced. From her longing she stopped, in order to touch the fake image. At the same time, on the other hand, the real James arrived. He saw Mandy and next to her, a boy same as him. Before he could ask who, it was, Mandy couldn't resist and ran to hug the tears. James screamed out from the depths of his soul a thunderous "NO", but it was too late. At once, the tear opened in two and sucked in the little girl. You could see her running around senseless. She had not understood what had happened; she was in her own world.

The hallucinations were produced by the fake James so that Mandy fell into his trap and keep her captivated forever. According to the rules of the city, anyone who touches one of the sacred tears is imprisoned forever and lives every day the biggest dream of his life over and over again so that he eventually goes mad. This is the punishment, because it is considered an immoral act to break a tear, because the world balance is being interrupted, since these are the tears of people who never shed for love. The tears that people keep inside themselves because they fear to love, to be loved and to hurt themselves. According to universal rules no one has the right to intervene in the life of an Earthman and overthrow it, because that would mean that alien creatures are dominant. Alien bodies just create the conditions for life, humans are the ones who live it.

Little Mandy, lost in a dream, was seeing herself and James running and playing around a large building with two floors and a garden as big as a park. She was turning around and round senselessly in the tear and laughed at herself.

James, bewildered, looked at himself across the street.

- Something strange is going on, James said to fake James. How can we be the same? Who are you?

-I am you, only created by witch Coumara, he told him. She saw you and your friend running in the ticking of the Great Clock, and instantly singled out the blood of mortals among the others. She also knows about the core of planet Pintura you have in your stomach. Do not forget that both you are guided by the same force. As you can see, you failed. You took Varvas' side and failed. Our stupid friend will stay here forever, and you are the one who is to blame. Unless…

- Unless what?

- Unless you give to Coumara the rest of the core. She will then release Mandy.

And just like that fake James became dust that fell down. James understood that Coumara had painted him since she could not herself enter Earth, in order to mislead Mandy. Now that she knew he was there; she would certainly try to ruin his plans. On the one hand, he was looking at Mandy running around like a fool and he was feeling despair, and on the other hand he had to fulfill his mission. He sat there all night watching his friend chasing herself and wondering what it was that she was seeing that made her so happy. It looked like the snowball that his dad once gifted him. It was from one of his business trips, and when he was shaking it, white snowflakes fell. A fake happiness. That's what exactly Mandy was feeling now.

James was trying to figure out how he would manage to save his friend without giving the core of planet Pintura to this filthy witch. Because something like that would mean the end of the world. But he couldn't leave little Mandy trapped in there. He looked at her and he saw how beautiful she looked in the water and realized how much he loved her. He would do anything to save her. Then, just before dawn, he fell asleep.

When he awoke, he was in an aquatic world. He was somewhere lost at the bottom of the ocean. Groups of countless fishes formed strange images in the water and Somewhere In between you could see James. The seabed was organized like a great state. Colorful plants formed large areas of parks for sea creatures to play and rest. Corals and shells tangled with concrete sand were the materials that the sea creatures used to build their houses. The houses didn't have any doors and they were open to all. Seaweed was hanging as curtains to drive away the light when the aquatics wanted to sleep. James thought that probably when he fell asleep the tearful ground of the city collapsed and so he found himself at the bottom of the sea. Opposite him there was a golden staircase leading back again. Apparently, the aquatics had predicted such incidents so that anyone who was at the bottom of sea accidentally could be able to turn back. James, however, thought that he could explore this world a little. So, he walked along the main street. Among the rocks a sign written in human handwriting was informing him that this was "The bright seabed", with a footnote "Please avoid swimming to the right side of the reef".

- What a nonsense, James thought! What harm can cause the right side? and with one move he began swimming towards it. Gradually, the waters were changing color. They turned into pink and peach, and the seabed looked so different. Full of colorful rocks from which protruded green and yellow precious stones. You could see around blossom lemon and orange trees. An unreal picture, as if they had trapped a piece of human Earth on this side of the seabed. Little mermaids came out and welcomed the visitor. They were talking to him in a language that James could not understand. It resembled the sounds of the sea, shrill and deep.

His thoughts were so far away from Mandy, from how he would save the world from Coumara's hands, from the mission he had to fulfill. He was enchanted by the beautiful atmosphere.

From above the witch who was watching him laughed and muttered,

- Ah, Varvas is so dumb, he trusted a mortal to save the Earth ... ha!

- You, stupid boy. Come here, she said to her faithful partner Silius. Do as we said to James. Exactly as I showed you, and she gave him her rickety brush. I'm going back to look for Varvas. He must be somewhere around here. Then the end of the Earth will come forever, I cannot wait another three months for the deadline that Sun has given to God Varvas to make amends. I want the dream of planet Hazair to finally come true, and I want it now!

That's what Kumara said and flew into the ether. Silius, without losing time, put the brush into the Earth and drew into the shape Coumara had already created. James at that same moment was entering a space that is not forbidden for ordinary mortals. The rock of Oblivion. Within the rock the colors of the sea seemed dull and indistinct. One could only discern slender figures of mermaids encircling him.

They surrounded James. Suddenly, out of nowhere, his dad appeared in front of him. James rolled his eyes and for a moment was bewildered. Then he ran to embrace him, even though something within his soul was telling him that something was wrong. Every time the boy reached his father's figure, he would slip away and then he was smiling at him defiantly. This smile seemed as if he was telling him that he could not reach him. James got even more stubborn and kept chasing him. This continued for days without stopping, until James got tired and fell down to rest. A mermaid, the most beautiful of the seabed, approached him and said:

- We want you to be our king. We will serve you faithfully if you remain here forever, and she placed a golden crown on his head. This is the life you were always dreaming of, next to your father as a king. You'll have anything you need.

James didn't say a word, he just followed the young mermaid to his throne. After he sat down, all the mermaids were embraced and howled joyfully. In front of him, the figure of his father was looking at him. James didn't care about anything anymore.

The mermaids every day would bring him the best food of the seabed, tended his hair, washed him, put him on the most expensive clothes and every night they read to him strange stories to sleep. It was pure happiness for them to have someone to look after, since they were doomed forever to never give birth to their own children. The mermaids who lived on the rock were cursed by witch Coumara. That's why the inhabitants of the ocean sent them there because they considered them defective beings.

James didn't understand much. His mind was stuck on his dad. He had stopped listening to his instinct, that voice within telling him that his dad had died.

Witch Coumara from above celebrated with Silius her great success. It had been almost two months since James was crowned king of the rock of Oblivion. In other words, only in a month from now the Earth would be hers. She no longer cared to spot God Varvas. The countdown had already begun. Everything had languished after all. Even Sun had ceased to shine. Each dawn seemed to him like a torture, while his anxiety for his son grew day by day. Everything was ready for the great fall. Unfortunately, in a month, the Earth would be completely surrendered into the hands of Coumara.

Somewhere behind the scenes, Life was returning to her house completely exhausted. She was travelling for many months. With the absence of God Varvas, it was Life who was trying to defend for the justice and wellbeing of people. When she arrived, her mind went straight to the flower that James had left her. The flower had rotted, and brown worms were coming out of it. Life realized that something terrible had happened. She immediately ran to the city of tears. She took her flying bicycle out of the storage room of her house and flew there. From above, her eye fell on the sacred building. She immediately saw Mandy trapped in a teardrop, running around. She looked as if she was the shadow of herself. Life got panicked. She searched for James but could not find him anywhere. After landing her bike on the tear-made ground she pulled out of her pocket her locator. With this device, Life could tell if the person she was looking for was close to her. The locator made the characteristic sound that meant that James was somewhere nearby. She looked around but could not see him anywhere. Suddenly the ground beneath her receded. And then she understood. James was underneath. Maybe he had reached the rock of Oblivion. She swam as fast as she could. All aquatic inhabitants made her way and bowed.

When she entered the rock, he saw James surrounded by beautiful mermaids entertaining him, and on the other side the fake, faded figure of his father. She immediately took a little sea sponge and extinguished it. James rolled his eyes at once. It was the first time that after two months he reacted into something. The mermaids turned to see what had happened. When they saw Life, they realized that the end of

James' reign had come and that they would be left alone again.

The most beautiful of them all, approached her and said:

- Please, Life, do not take him from us. You have already forgotten us, do not take us now the only gift you gave us.

Before Life could answer, James got up from his throne, shook off the crown and hugged the brunette mermaid.

- Do not worry. Life may have forgotten you, but I will never forget you. I have to leave, but I promise I'll be back. And they hugged all together in an emotional atmosphere.

Chapter 9

A month before the end of the world

James climbed the golden ladder silent. He was incredibly ashamed that he let his feelings carry him away. He felt so stupid.

When they reached the surface, James asked how much time was left. Life, who had realized how bad the little one was feeling, responded:

- One month, my child. With a clever plan, and proper implementation you stand great chances to save the world. But still it does not benefit anyone to blame yourself. You are human and, although you have God Varvas inside you, you have weaknesses and flaws. It was expected to fall into the witch's trap. Your human side prevailed you. Coumara relied on that. But I believe in you. You have something valuable, other than the gift God sent you. You know how to fight, and that's the most important thing of all. I have to leave you now because the chaos on Earth is evolving. Have a good trip, my little one. Do not be afraid to reach until the end of your destination.

And just like that Life rode her bike and left.

James, after wandering in the City of Tears, which had completely changed since the last time he was there, sat outside the sacred building looking at Mandy. He knelt and shouted at her:

- I will do everything I can to save you.

Then he continued walking his lonely path. After passing the city boarders, he ran on a wooden bridge that was hovering in the air. There were only clouds around him. He closed his eyes and walked like that for many hours, having in his mind shattered images of the seabed, his mom, his dad and of Mandy's.

When he opened them, the Kingdom of Time had begun to show faintly.

Two clock hands welcomed him to the strange city. Anywhere he could turn his head, he could see clocks: small and large. Scenes from people's lives were showing between the clocks. As if they were showing in big, glass spheres. They looked like the screens of big movies. Yesterday, tomorrow and now, it was all in there. The extent of the city was endless. James kept walking to find the place where his and his family's life was. He walked along the clocks and saw the misery of the world. The Earth was being destroyed. Every household was mourning over a new calamity. After days of wandering he reached the right place. On the screen he saw his mom with Mandy's parents, unhappy, looking for their children. They had looked everywhere but they couldn't find anything. The only clue they had was the colors in James' room, but this wasn't able to lead them anywhere. The human mind cannot comprehend the existence of another world like the one on the other side of the planet.

Just a few steps away, the screen was showing his dad down the street, full of blood. It was the day of the accident. His dad was on his way to watch his son play basketball. The screen had stopped there and showed nothing else. James took out his brush and painted a button on the screen. He pressed it and the screen started running backwards. When he reached the spot just before the accident, he stopped it. Unable to bear the emotions that overwhelmed him, he sat down and cried, as he had never cried in his life.

After two hours he set off for his destination: the center of the Earth. The trip lasted three days because James, exhausted and sad, often took breaks where he painted something to eat and then got up again. Throughout the journey he painted flowers and trees to beautify the landscape. He arrived by the dawn. It was a very sacred place. The center of the Earth consisted of a round circle. People were standing around it with open arms. Each person represented a different nation on Earth. Each one was chosen by God Varvas and remained there to protect their nation and defend their interests peacefully. Somewhere nearby was his dad's red thread. This is the placc whcrc all the lost things of the universe go. He asked an Englishman if he had seen her. He responded negatively but offered to help him. Gradually, all the people left the circle and together with James, were looking for the red thread of his father.

They were searching all day long and during the night. The next morning the Italian representative found it. He put it in a glass box and handed it to James. Only nine days remained before the end of the month, so James had to hurry up. He thanked the chosen ones and headed back again.

Coumara from above, had just realized that James had escaped the rock of Oblivion. She was quite busy with the disasters and misery she was painting on Earth and so sure that the case was closed that she had forgot all about James.

When she saw him, she got so angry that she immediately drew a thunderbolt that struck to the tree, next to James. Fortunately, she failed. James started running scared. He had to reach the Kingdom of Time as soon as possible. Coumara, meanwhile, did not give up. She continued painting lightnings and thunders all the way, while he was running like a maniac to avoid them. This went on for the rest of the day until Coumara got tired of chasing him. Besides, he was not able to do anything to her. In eight days, it would all be over for him and for the rest of humanity. It was already midnight when James arrived in the Kingdom again. He stood in front of his dad's paused screen and threw the red thread on it. The screen immediately shone strangely. Then he synchronized the countless screens at the same time and date. A year ago, so that human life on the planet is in balance with time. The whole procedure took him three days, since the number of screens is equal to the total number of inhabitants of the Earth.

And so, on Earth the move, the speech, the life stopped. No one talked, they did not walk, did not run. Everyone and everything were immovable. Fortunately, Coumara was missing in her hometown Kazan to collect coumarins, so she did not notice the change. Her partner Silius, didn't realize the change also, as he had fallen asleep instead of watching the Earth, But Sun immediately noticed the big difference. Suddenly the noise, the laughter and crying stopped. He thought that it was Coumara's plan, so he did not pay any attention. He had resigned. Before pressing the start button to play life on Earth again, James had to return himself and Mandy to the positions they were at the time. It was easy for him since Life would radiate him easily. But Mandy was trapped in the sacred tear, so she would be imprisoned forever. His mind was about to explode. What should he do? He let the day pass sitting in front of the glass sphere of Mandy's life, skeptical. She was wearing her orange dress and seemed anxious for the game. He had to come up with something.

Meanwhile, Coumara, returning from Kazan, flew with her broomstick above the Earth. She realized that something strange was happening. This is James' work. Of course, she could not understand what this was all about. So, she stood over the Kingdom of Time and saw him asleep in front of the clocks. Now she had the chance to kill him. But then she thought that if she killed him, the rest of the core of planet Pintura would be lost with him, and that was something she did not like at all. She always thought that one day the core would end up to her hands and the she'd become omnipotent. She needed time to decide about James' fate, so she transferred him to planet Kazan. With her brush, she painted awful black nets and trapped him in them. Then he pulled them up and pulled them off the surface of the Earth. She tied the nets with the sleeping James on her dirty broomstick and transferred him to Kazan.

When the little one woke up and saw this new planet, he thought that he was still asleep, dreaming of the worst nightmare of his life. All he could see was a huge area with scorched soil and rotten arbutus trees and coumarins. The trees were the only element that distinguished the dry ground from the black sky. Awful rotten creatures, reminiscent of human beings were picking up rotten coumarins and placing them in boxes, while two of them were guarding him. He wanted to talk to someone to find out what had happened. But no one replied his questions. Their eyes were empty, and they seemed as if they weren't feeling anything around them.

Suddenly the rotten organisms left the coumarin harvest and fell down. James turned around and saw the ugliest creature of his life. It was witch Coumara.

- Did you wake up?

- Where am I? he asked full of wonder and fear.

- You are in Kazan, you idiot. You thought you could save the world. Hahaha. In three days, the Earth will become mine. I do not understand one thing only: Why did you stop Life on Earth? Anyway, it does not matter, because that way you make my work easier. Hahaha.

And Coumara ate two coumarins from the ground.

- What do you want from me? Why did you bring me here?

- You should be feeling grateful that I haven't killed you! I will keep you here as long as I want. Do you see these fools? she said and pointed to the fallen rotten beings. They pretended to be heroes like you, and this is where they ended up. People are so stupid.

Before James answered her, the witch had already ridden her broomstick and was flying away. The little one was already in despair. The planet would be destroyed in three days and he was the one to blame. He had to think of something new. But all he could think of was Mandy. He could not take it any longer and burst into tears. He cried for hours until he looked down. The soil he had watered with his tears had begun to bloom.

- This is it! James thought and took out his brush. Suddenly he painted the sleep on the rotten beings, and they fell asleep. Then he took his colors and started mixing them for hours. When he achieved the right portion, he colored all the coumarins that suddenly turned red and juicy. Then he sat down and was waiting for Coumara. As soon as she realized her presence, she pretended to be asleep. Coumara approached the coumarins. Never in her life had she seen such juicy fruits. Her longing to eat them was so great that she could not wait a moment. With one move she began to devour as many coumarins as she could.

Gradually her face began to change, she was looking beautiful. The black balls she had instead of eyes gave way to a turquoise, melancholy look and her hair flared so much that her hat could not hold the wave of curls that flowed from her head. James had painted Love. The thing that what was missing for so many years from the witch's life. Suddenly Coumara started to cry. She cried for two days and nights. She wept for all those who had never cried, for all the disasters she had caused and the evil she had bring to people. And something really shocking happened in the City of Tears. The tears of the holy temple began to crack and then break, just like the tear-made floor. Everything became a big tear that was absorbed by the sand and the soil. The water that watered the Earth transformed the City of Tears into a city with millions of species of vegetation. Trees, flowers and grass everywhere. And ever since then the City of Tears was renamed Thiapolis and was the most beautiful part of the Earth.

From this terrible flood the creatures that were trapped in the teardrops could hardly survive…

Seeing the disaster, Silius immediately rushed to Kazan to inform Coumara. When he saw her, he barely recognized her.

- Master Coumara, is that you?

- Yes, my dear Silius, it's me. What happened?

Silius could not believe his own eyes. The witch had changed so much and although he was always in love with her, now he felt even more for her.

-Don't start screaming but something very strange happened. The City of Tears broke and flooded. And the teardrops were replaced with tropical vegetation. Some of our prisoners were released and some others died.

- Do not worry, believe me, Silius. I'm going to see what happened. You go to Sun and tell him that I am relinquishing the sovereignty of the Earth. The only one who deserves to have this position is God Varvas.

James, who had heard their conversation, told the witch to take him immediately to Thiapolis. He had to find Mandy. The witch, flooded with thousands of emotions, accepted immediately. And because her broomstick fell apart, soaked in hatred, they both took out their brushes and started painting a rainbow that ended up on Earth. Full of anxiety, James ran over it as fast as he could. Coumara also followed him, running. For the first time in her life she felt so free.

When they arrived, James could not recognize the city. Coumara too. She didn´t enter the city, as she was not allowed but she looked at it from above. It was an earthly paradise. Full of green. Spring seemed to have finally found its home. Little dwarfs emerged behind the green trees. They were the imprisoned beings of the City of Tears.

They proceeded to Lillypolis, the place where the survivors had placed the dead people after the fall. A flower had sprouted next to each victim. It symbolized their soul.

James saw a beautiful white lily. Carved with fuchsia and orange details. He approached the flower to admire its beauty. He wondered who had such a beautiful soul. And underneath he saw little Mandy. Distressed and exhausted. He bent down and kissed her. Then he burst into tears. He was the one to blame for everything. Coumara was telling him from above that it was not his fault. She was crying too.

In the ethers, Mandy's soul found herself on a bright path that led to the realm of souls, where all the dead people go. She kept going until he met a strange figure. He was very familiar to her, but she could not understand who she was. When their eyes met, the strange figure asked:

-What are you doing here? Why aren't you with James?

-How do you know James? Who are you?

-I'm God Varvas' soul. I'm here because my body is into a comma.

-So, you are God Varvas! But what has happened? Will you explain to me?

Then God Varvas began to narrate to her how he accidentally killed James' father, how Coumara ruled the Earth and how James became God Varvas.

On the other side of the universe, Silius informed the celestial bodies about the change of Coumara and her decision to resign, after the intervention of James. Sun could not believe in his ears that a mortal had entered the other side of the Earth.

-But who gave him the permission for something like that?

Then Asterius thought it was the right time to tell everyone what he had seen that night. Altogether, led by Sun, they ran to the place where the body of God Varvas was.

Sun, seeing the God lying down, fell on top of him, shouting:

- My son, my son, wake up.

God Varvas stayed still, without responding.

-Bring me the mortal and Coumara immediately, he ordered.

Silius ran to the rainbow and before entering Thiapolis he found them tangled in a tangle of tears.

-Sun ordered me to follow me into the skies immediately, he told them. God Varvas was found in a coma. They need you right away.

When they arrived, everyone was looking at them strangely. They had never seen a mortal face-to-face. Nobody recognized witch Coumara. She had to say who she was to stop everyone looking at her like a stranger. Sun, who was thinking only of God Varvas, said to them:

-Please join your palms and paint a ladder to return my son's soul back. Otherwise, I will lose him too.

James, terrified, looked at him intently. He did not believe that he was in heaven and that he was talking to Sun.

Coumara told him:

- Don't worry, we will do everything possible to get him back. He does not deserve to end like this.

Immediately the witch and little James, took out their brushes. It took them two days and nights to finish the staircase to the bright path that was the soul of the God. When they arrived, Varvas was sitting on the white floor.

Coumara approached him and caressed his shoulder.

- Who are you? he told her.

- You haven't recognized me yet? I'm the ugliest witch of all times, Coumara.

God Varvas was staring at her to find in her face some connection with the past, but he couldn't.

- But what happened? The earth? James' father?

Coumara and James sat down and explained everything to him, and God Varvas felt very proud of the little one. He did not imagine that a mortal could do what he had not been able to do for so many centuries, to change witch Coumara.

Then Coumara said:

- Let's go. James and I came to bring you back. Sun is very worried.

- I cannot leave. We have to do something with Mandy. She was here and we talked for days until she was sucked into the realm of souls because she was obviously late to enter.

- What, Mandy was here? James said. But how did you let her go? Can't we get into the realm? Should we paint a door there and go in and get her?

- I wish it was so easy, but the sphere of souls is protected by a very strong energy field. No one can pass it and reach the crust of the sphere.

- Let's go back, said Coumara. By the time we'll return we will figure it out.

Chapter 10

The end

So, they all went down the stairs together. The sky was full of stars. They had all come out to welcome God Varvas. James was looking at the stars one by one on the way and they were smiling at him. When they reached the universe, the soul of the God next to his body became transparent. He lay on his body and became one again. Soul and body were reunited. Coumara and James hurried to heal his wounds with their brushes. And after two hours God Varvas woke up.

Above him Sun shone full of agony. As soon as he opened his eyes, he hugged him tightly. The same did the rest of the universe. James was sitting stunned and looking at them. After the joyful event, a council was convened to decide what should be done with Mandy, James and the Earth that had been completely immobilized.

Varvas spoke first and said:

- I suggest that we restart the Earth from the point where it has stopped. As I had planned initially with James. But without Mandy. Mandy should be erased. As if she never existed. And she will be born again when James reaches ten years old. So, we will have two years ahead of us to restore the Earth from the disasters and erase the traces of Mandy so that no one understands the slightest thing.

-And how will this happen, James asked.

-We will go back in time, just before Mandy was born, and you will erase her with my intergalactic eraser. Then you too must let me erase from your head your memories with the little one but also the images you saw on this long journey. No mortal should know about us. But in order to do all this you have to give me back the core of planet Pintura.

- What exactly are you going to do to me? James asked scared.

- I will have to open your belly to get my stomach out of you. Coumara will help me in this too.

- Agreed, said the witch.

But James could not hide his fear. God Varvas approached him and said in his ear:

- Do not be afraid. I would never let anything bad happen to you. You are a part of me now.

Then they sent James back to the Kingdom of Time to return Mandy's life to its beginning. He took out the galactic eraser for the last time and just before erasing it forever from his life, he whispered: "Goodbye my little one. I will wait for you to come and find me." And simple as that, he erased it. He also went to the screens of the little girl's relatives and friends and erased her from there as well.

Thus, Mandy's soul flew from the sphere of souls to the glassy white earth. This is the place where the unborn people's souls are staying. Human souls when being born on

Earth have no memory of this form of life, so there is no danger of revealing the existence of galactic beings.

Behind the scenes of the Earth, little James passed by the house of Life to say goodbye to her but also to guide her to press the button to start life on Earth again.

James ran over her and hugged her.

- Goodbye Life, he told her. The journey is over for me. And the painting.

- Goodbye my little one. Do not worry, your journey will continue and will last a long time. As for the painting, it never ends. In fact, Life is nothing more than a piece of white paper. You have the colors in your hands.

James smiled. He did not understand exactly what Life meant but it sounded beautiful to him. Before leaving, he conveyed Varvas' orders for the button to the Kingdom of Time. Life greeted him, knowing that the little one would no longer be the same after all this. The divine gift given to him by God Varvas would accompany him for the rest of his life and would make him different from all the others around him. Because planet Pintura may have been taken away from him, but the remnants of the God would remain in him forever.

Then, James began returning back. He looked at the stars as he ascended into the universe. It was the last time he could see them so closely. He wanted to leave something of his own in the sky, his personal mark that will reveal that he was once there. He took out his brush and made a huge, glowing M in the sky, dedicated to his little friend. Could she be able to see that when she would return to her normal life?

With the thought of his friend, little James, reached the clouds again/ God and the witch were waiting for him. Before Coumara painted the sleep on his eyes, James turned to God Varvas and said to him:

-Please find the mermaids of the rock of Oblivion and help them. I promised them.

With just one move of the witch, James fell asleep. Varvas painted a magical passage in the little boy's hand and in his own. He lay down next to him and joined their hands tightly. A red light began to run with force from the child's belly to his hand and then the light passed into Varvas' body. The hands of the |God refilled colors. At once he took out his eraser and erased from James' mind all the memories from his trip but also Mandy. But he could not erase the feelings that created him. Gods have access only to the human's minds, not to their hearts.

After the witch and the God let him sleep for hours, they took James' body and placed it on a glossy slide made of sugar and red paint. Coumara pushed him gently from behind and the little one returned to Earth, back to the day of the accident. Everything was ready. Varvas signaled to Life and she pressed the start button. The Earth began to spin again. The cosmic beings were celebrating, and Sun was smiling again. Democracy was happy too. Everything would be fine.

At the same time, James opened his eyes and scored. His team had won thanks to him. He turned to the stands and saw his dad applauding him with pride. Next to him an orange balloon escaped from a little girl and ascended to the sky. The little one looked up and felt very strange, until his teammates reached him and brought him back to the celebrations.

Varvas was looking down and was smiling. Then he entered the white earth to talk to Mandy.

She was sitting in a white hammock when she realized his presence in the room.

She ran and hugged him. She took a photo from her pocket and gave it to him. It was him in the hands of Goddess Salva. He had met her in the realm of souls and the goddess gave it to her to her when Mandy was leaving for the white earth.

-Your mom is very beautiful, she told him. The most beautiful woman I have ever seen. You look a lot like her.

God Varvas took it in his arms and thanked her. They then sat in the hammock and he informed her about everything and especially about James. Mandy was happy until she was announced that she would have to wait two years to return to Earth. He blushed immediately. She already missed her parents and her friend. God Varvas promised her that he would visit her very often and that he would teach her all the secrets of painting. Indeed, he did so. Every Friday, God Varvas took Mandy's soul and traveled it to the ends of the Galaxy. He gave her his brush and she was making the most beautiful things she could think of, always according to his instructions. Most of all, she enjoyed creating weird designs using the clouds. Animals, flowers, waves. Everything she was missing from Earth she captured them in the clouds. This went on for two years until it was time for Mandy to return to Earth. God Varvas had everything prepared. He had erased all her traces and restored the Earth to its early form. The planet was smiling again.

Mandy grabbed the God by the neck and kissed him with all her might.

-Thank you, God Varvas, for everything. I will continue to paint on Earth, just for you. Take care of me and make strange images for me with the clouds.

Then she disappeared, because in a hospital on Earth Mandy had just been born.

God Varvas sat on the fuchsia goodbye that Mandy had painted for him. He looked so sad. Coumara immediately went to comfort him. They had become very good friends these two years. Maybe something more.

Down on Earth the years were passing by. James and Mandy were growing up so close to each other, in the same neighborhood, but without knowing each other, without knowing how much they had in common. They both showed a great love for painting, without understanding what they were motivated by.

God Varvas looked down on them and was really proud of them. He had now taken on the task of educating his son, the magician Varmaro.

Thus, twenty years passed since the day that Mandy returned to Earth. Mankind was now prospering. The couple Varvas-Coumara took extra care for the happiness of the Earth. In fact, they reorganized planet Kazan to make it habitable for humans in the future. A part of the other side of the Earth had become known to the human beings, after God Varvas' intervention. It was decided by law that all mortals could enter Thiapolis. But they could not perceive the presence of the magical creatures that lived there. Like the mermaids of the rock of Oblivion for example. They also lived there after the destruction of the City of Tears, in a huge swimming pool. This was the gift of God Varvas to them. They watched James growing up and were really proud of him, since he often went to Thiapolis to paint. He considered it a sacred place, without knowing why. Just like Mandy. She spent hours fooling around with the strange designs of the clouds. It was God Varvas, who was creating them for her. From that place she could see better than anywhere else a distinct star formation that resembled the original of her name. M.

An unsuspected Sunday afternoon, James and Mandy, all grownups now were in the same place, at the same time. The clouds suddenly looked like fireworks exploding in the bare sky. Unprecedented music was played by secret accords of nature. When their eyes met strange emotions overwhelmed them both. An orange balloon flew out of nowhere. The miracle had happened at last. And the planet was smiling like never before.

About the author

Marilena Pappa is a Greek author. Born in Athens in 1988, she studied Public Administration at Panteion University and Communications and Journalism. She has been working in the field of Public Relations, Communication, Marketing and Advertising since 2013 in Publishing Houses, Advertising agencies and Organizations. She has published books for children, poetry collections and literature for adults in Greece and Cyprus, while she has translated children´s books from English to Greek. She was nominated for Best Children's Book in Cyprus´ State Literature Awards in 2013. Her children's book "James & The smiling planet" that has originally published under the title "Ο πλανήτης που χαμογελά" in 2010 has been transferred as a theatrical play. She has collaborated with cultural websites as a columnist, writing book and theatrical reviews.

Find more: **marilenapappa.com**